3 MINUTE
BEDTIME STORIES

Retold by Gina Phillips

Illustrated by F.S. Persico

SMITHMARK

Copyright © 1992 Kidsbooks Inc.
7004 N. California Ave.
Chicago, IL 60645

ISBN: 0-8317-2592-3

This edition published in 1992 by SMITHMARK Publishers Inc.,
112 Madison Avenue, New York, NY 10016

SMITHMARK books are available for bulk purchase for sales promotion and premium use.
For details write or telephone the Manager of Special Sales, SMITHMARK Publishers Inc.,
112 Madison Avenue, New York, NY 10016. (212) 532-6600.
Manufactured in the United States of America

Goldilocks and the Three Bears

Once upon a time there were three bears—a big papa bear, a medium-sized mama bear, and a wee baby bear. They lived in a house in the middle of the forest. Every day Mama Bear made porridge for breakfast. One morning, while the porridge was cooling down so they could eat it, the bear family decided to take a walk.

While they were gone a little girl who was lost in the forest came upon the empty house. Her name was Goldilocks. She knocked on the door, but there was no answer, so she just turned the knob and went inside.

Goldilocks smelled the steaming bowls of porridge and began to feel very hungry indeed. First she tasted the porridge in the big bowl that belonged to Papa Bear, but it was too hot. Next she tried the porridge in the medium-sized bowl that was Mama Bear's, but it was too cold. Then she tasted the porridge in the little bowl that belonged to Baby Bear, and it was just right. So she ate it all up.

After Goldilocks finished eating, she decided to rest. First she climbed on Papa Bear's big chair, but it was too hard. Next she tried Mama Bear's chair, but it was too soft. Then she sat in Baby Bear's chair, but she was too heavy and the chair broke into pieces.

Then Goldilocks went upstairs and saw three beds. She felt tired and decided to take a nap. First she tried the big bed, but it was too hard. The middle-sized bed was far too soft. But when she tried the littlest bed it was just right. Goldilocks snuggled under the covers and fell fast asleep.

A short time later the bears returned from their walk. Papa Bear looked at his bowl and roared, "SOMEBODY HAS BEEN EATING MY PORRIDGE!" Then Mama Bear said in her gentle voice, "Somebody has been eating my porridge, too."

Then Baby Bear looked at his empty bowl and cried in a tiny voice, "Somebody has been eating my porridge and ate it all up!"

Next the bears looked at their chairs. "SOMEBODY HAS BEEN SITTING IN MY CHAIR!" roared Papa Bear. Mama Bear saw the rumpled cushions on her chair and said in her gentle voice, "Somebody has been sitting in my chair, too." Then Baby Bear saw his chair and sobbed, "Somebody has been sitting in my chair and has broken it into pieces!"

The three bears hurried upstairs and looked into their bedroom. Papa Bear saw that his pillow had been moved and roared, "SOMEBODY HAS BEEN SLEEPING IN MY BED!" Mama Bear gently said, "Somebody has been sleeping in my bed, too." Then Baby Bear looked at his bed and said, "Somebody has been sleeping in my bed and here she is!"

At that moment Goldilocks woke up. She saw the three bears standing around her and jumped out of the bed, ran down the stairs, and out of the house. And the three bears never saw Goldilocks again.

The Ugly Duckling

Each spring a mother duck laid her eggs in the reeds by a lake and sat on them faithfully. One day the ducklings hatched, except for one. "My, this egg is so big! Why doesn't it hatch?" said the mother duck. She sat back down and waited. Finally there was a loud crack and out popped the last duckling. "Goodness! He is so gray and ugly!" cried the mother duck. "But he is my child and I will love him just the same."

When the mother duck led her babies to the water for a swim, the big ugly duckling swam better than his brothers and sisters. Afterward, the mother duck proudly brought her children to the farmyard to meet the other animals. All the little ducklings were praised and admired, except for the ugly duckling. The animals were unkind and teased him cruelly. Some even bit him!

The ugly duckling was so miserable that one day he decided to run away. Without even saying good-bye, he left the nest in the reeds and headed for a big marsh. "No one can pick on me here," said the ugly duckling sadly, as he looked around the huge gloomy place.

The next morning some wild ducks swam up to the ugly duckling. "My, you certainly are ugly," they said, "but we can be friends anyway." The ugly duckling was happy to have some company and they swam along together and dove for fish. Suddenly there was a loud bang. Bang! Bang! "Oh, no," said the wild ducks. "The hunters have come with their dogs and guns! We must leave at once!" The wild ducks flew away in the blink of an eye. The frightened duckling froze in his place when a hunting dog ran up to him. But the dog just sniffed at him and bounded past. The duckling was glad to be spared but he thought, "I'm so ugly, not even a hunting dog wants me." And he sadly swam away.

Summer passed and autumn came. The duckling was miserable and lonely. One evening he looked up and saw some beautiful white birds with long necks flying overhead. They made unusual sounds. Suddenly the ugly duckling let out a sharp honk that was so loud and full of longing that he scared himself. "Who are those birds?" he wondered. But before he could call out to them again, the birds flew past and the ugly duckling was alone once more.

The winter was bitter and the poor ugly duckling nearly froze to death. But somehow he survived the cold and loneliness.

One day the following spring, the ugly duckling was flying high in the air when he saw three white, long-necked birds floating on the lake below him. They were so lovely, he was drawn to them and flew down and settled on the water nearby. Thinking they were going to tease him and drive him off because he was so ugly, the duckling bowed his head. At that moment he saw his reflection in the water. "Is that me?" he asked in surprise. To his amazement, the ugly duckling saw that he had beautiful white feathers and a long graceful neck. Just like the other birds nearby!

"Look at the new swan! He is more beautiful than any of the others," shouted some children standing near the water's edge. The other swans swam up to him and nodded their heads in approval. The young swan's heart filled with joy. "I never imagined that an ugly duckling like me could grow up to be so beautiful." And for the rest of his days the swan brought happiness to all who saw him.

The Gingerbread Boy

Once there was an old woman and an old man who wanted a child very much. But since they had none, the old woman decided to make a little boy out of gingerbread. She put the dough on a cookie sheet and slid it into the oven.

After a while she smelled the gingerbread baking and went to see if it was done. When she opened the oven door, out popped the gingerbread boy and away he ran, right out of the house. The old man and the old woman tried to catch him, but the boy just shouted, "Run, run, as fast as you can; you can't catch me, I'm the gingerbread man!"

As the gingerbread boy ran down the road he passed a cow who mooed, "You look much tastier than the grass I'm eating." And the cow started to chase him, too.

"Oh, ho," said the gingerbread boy, "I've run away from an old man and an old woman. Run, run, as fast as you can; you can't catch me, I'm the gingerbread man!" And away he went.

Next he came to a horse who called out, "I'd like to eat you!" And the horse started trotting after the gingerbread boy.

"I've run away from an old man and an old woman and a cow! Run, run, as fast as you can; you can't catch me, I'm the gingerbread man!" And away he went.

The gingerbread boy ran into a meadow, where he came upon some mowers. When the mowers saw the delicious-looking gingerbread boy they cried, "Stop! Stop! You were made to be eaten!"

But the gingerbread boy said, "I've run away from an old man and an old woman, a cow, and a horse. Run, run, as fast as you can; you can't catch me, I'm the gingerbread man!" Then the gingerbread boy ran into the woods, where he came upon a fox. "Don't try to catch me," warned the gingerbread boy. "I've run away from an old man and an old woman, a cow, a horse, and some mowers. Run, run, as fast as you can; you can't catch me, I'm the gingerbread man!"

The fox told the gingerbread boy he had no reason to catch him, as he had just finished eating a big lunch. At this moment the gingerbread boy saw a large stream in front of him and asked the fox how he could cross it. "I shall be glad to take you across on my back," the fox offered.

The gingerbread boy was very happy. He jumped onto the fox's back and the fox started swimming. As the water got deeper the gingerbread boy's feet got wet, so the fox said, "Why don't you jump up on my nose?" The gingerbread boy, glad to get away from the water, did exactly that. But as he jumped the fox opened his jaws wide and—snip, snap!—ate the gingerbread boy in two bites. After all, that's exactly what gingerbread boys are made for—to be eaten!

Little Red Riding Hood

There once was a little girl who lived at the edge of the forest. She always wore a red cape with a red hood that her grandmother had made for her, so everyone called her Little Red Riding Hood.

One day Little Red Riding Hood's mother asked her to take a basket of food to her sick grandmother, who lived on the other side of the forest.

Little Red Riding Hood was happy to go. As she walked through the woods she stopped to pick some flowers. Suddenly a wolf appeared. "Hello, little girl," said the wolf. "Where are you going with that basket?"

"I'm bringing some cakes to my sick grandmother who lives on the other side of the forest," replied the girl.

The sly wolf said good-bye and quickly raced through the forest to the grandmother's house. He knocked softly on the door.

"Who is it?" called the old woman from her bed.

"It is your granddaughter, Little Red Riding Hood," said the wolf in his softest voice. Fooled by the wolf's disguised voice, the grandmother opened the door and was promptly eaten by the wolf. The wolf then put on her nightgown and nightcap and climbed into bed to wait for Little Red Riding Hood.

Soon there was a knock at the door. "Who is it?" asked the wolf ever so gently.

"It is your granddaughter," said Little Red Riding Hood.

"Come in, my dear," replied the wolf. Little Red Riding Hood thought her grandmother sounded strange, but decided it was because she was ill. But when the girl stood next to the bed, she noticed that her grandmother looked a little different, too.

"Grandmother," she said, "what big eyes you have."

The wolf grinned and said, "All the better to see you with, my dear."

"My, my, Grandmother! What big ears you have!" said Little Red Riding Hood.

"All the better to hear you with, my dear," answered the wolf.

When Little Red Riding Hood noticed the wolf's sharp teeth, she said, "Grandmother, what big teeth you have!"

"All the better to eat you with, my dear!" shouted the wolf as he threw off the covers and sprang out of bed. Little Red Riding Hood ran from the wolf. Just as the wolf was about to catch her the door burst open. A hunter had heard the girl's cries. He aimed his gun and killed the wolf.

Little Red Riding Hood was happy to have been saved, but she was very sad about losing her grandmother. The hunter slit open the wolf's body, and much to Little Red Riding Hood's joy, out jumped her grandmother safe and sound. She was very happy to see Little Red Riding Hood, who gave her grandmother the basket of food and the flowers she had picked.

And from that time on, Little Red Riding Hood never again stopped to talk to wolves when she walked through the forest.

Henny Penny

One day, while Henny Penny was in the barnyard pecking at some grain, an acorn dropped down and hit her right on the head.

"Goodness me!" said Henny Penny. "The sky is falling! I must run and tell the king!" She hurried along until she met Cocky Locky.

"Where are you going, Henny Penny?" asked Cocky Locky.

"I have to tell the king the sky is falling!" cried Henny Penny.

"I'll go with you," said Cocky Locky. And Cocky Locky ran along with Henny Penny until they met Ducky Lucky.

"Where are you two going?" asked Ducky Lucky.

"We have to tell the king the sky is falling!" said Henny Penny.

"I'll go, too!" said Ducky Lucky. So all three ran to tell the king. Soon they met Goosey Loosey.

"Where are all of you going?" asked Goosey Loosey.

"We're going to tell the king the sky is falling!" they answered all together.

"My! I'll come, too," said Goosey Loosey as he joined the others. Next they met Turkey Lurkey.

"Where is everyone going?" asked Turkey Lurkey.

"To tell the king the sky is falling!" shouted all of the animals.

"I'll go with you," said Turkey Lurkey. They kept running until they met Foxy Loxy.

"Where are you going?" asked Foxy Loxy.

"We're going to tell the king the sky is falling," answered Henny Penny.

"Really? Well, you're going the wrong way," said Foxy Loxy. "Follow me. I know the right way."

10

"Thank you, Foxy Loxy," said Henny Penny, Cocky Locky, Ducky Lucky, Goosey Loosey, and Turkey Lurkey. So Foxy Loxy led them through the forest to a cave. It was really the entrance to his den. "This is a shortcut to the king's palace. It's dark, so I'll go first," said Foxy Loxy, licking his lips.

Foxy Loxy went into his den and waited for Henny Penny, Cocky Locky, Ducky Lucky, Goosey Loosey, and Turkey Lurkey to follow.

Henny Penny was just about to go in when she remembered she had some chores to do at home. "I must be going," said Henny Penny as she turned and started for the barnyard. Just then, Cocky Locky, Ducky Lucky, Goosey Loosey, and Turkey Lurkey all remembered that they, too, had errands to run and other things to do. "Foxy Loxy knows the way to the palace," said Goosey Loosey. "Let him tell the king that the sky is falling." At that, all of them turned and ran to catch up with Henny Penny.

So Henny Penny and her friends lived happily ever after. Foxy Loxy went hungry that day, and all of them forgot all about telling the king that the sky was falling.

Once there was an old woman and her son, Jack. They were very poor, so poor that in order to live they had to sell everything they owned except for their cow. But the day soon came when the cow had to be sold, too.

As Jack walked the cow to the market a strange man approached him and said, "What a good cow. I have no money, but I do have some magic beans. I'll trade them for your cow."

The beans looked ordinary, but the man insisted that they had special powers, so Jack agreed to the trade. When he went home and told his mother what had happened, she cried angrily, "You have been tricked. Now we have nothing!" And she tossed the beans out the window.

The next morning, when Jack looked out his window, he was astonished to see a beanstalk so tall it disappeared into the clouds. He began to climb it.

When he reached the top Jack saw a tremendous castle. He crept up to it and quietly slipped inside through a large crack in a wall. Inside there was an enormous table and chair. Suddenly Jack heard thundering footsteps. He hid behind a door as a huge giant holding a club stormed into the room. "Fe, fi, fo, fum! I smell the blood of an Englishman!" roared the giant.

"That's just your dinner," said the giant's wife, carrying in an enormous plate and setting it on the table. Jack shook with fear as the giant sat down and began to eat. Next the woman brought a goose and a golden harp. The giant looked at the goose and roared, "Lay!" The goose immediately laid an egg of solid gold. Then the giant looked at the harp. "Play!" he commanded. The magic harp played all by itself, and kept playing until the giant fell asleep.

"With that goose we would never be poor again," Jack thought. "What a gift that harp would be for my mother." Ever so quietly Jack climbed up the table leg and grabbed the harp and the goose under his arm. Then he slid down and headed for the door. Suddenly the harp began to play loudly. The giant woke up and growled, "Fe, fi, fo, fum! I smell the blood of an Englishman!"

Jack raced back to the beanstalk and quickly began climbing down. The bellowing giant followed close behind. Jack's mother heard all the noise and ran outside their house. Jack called to her for an axe.

His mother handed Jack the axe just as he touched the ground. With one mighty chop, Jack slashed through the beanstalk and the giant crashed to the earth.

Jack and his mother kept the magic goose and the golden harp and were never poor again.

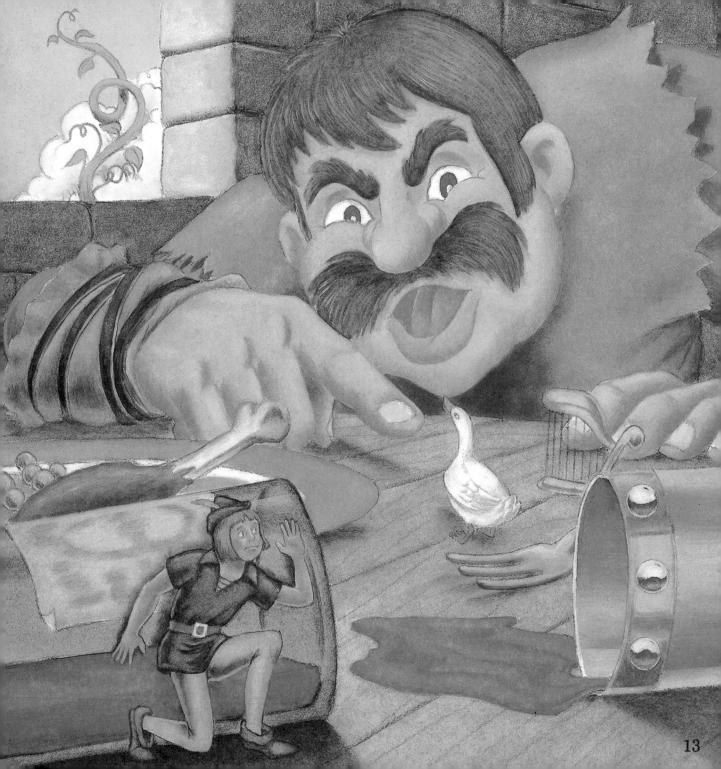

Sleeping Beauty

One day in a faraway land a princess was born. The king and queen had waited a long time for this child and were overjoyed at her birth. Everyone in the land, including twelve fairies, was invited to a celebration. Each fairy brought a different blessing for the baby princess. But before the last one could bestow her gift, a thirteenth fairy burst into the room. Furious at not being invited, the wicked fairy said, "My gift is a curse! When the princess is sixteen, she will prick her finger on a spindle and die!"

But the fairy who had not yet bestowed her gift spoke up and said, "No, the princess will not die but will sleep for a hundred years and be awakened by the kiss of a handsome prince." The king ordered every spindle in the land to be burned that very day.

The princess grew more beautiful and clever as the years passed and was beloved by everyone. On her sixteenth birthday the princess was wandering through the castle when she came upon an old woman spinning yarn. The old woman had never heard the king's order to destroy all the spindles.

Curious, for she had never seen such a thing as a spindle, the princess asked if she could hold it. But the instant she touched it, she pricked her finger and fell into a deep sleep.

The fairies caused a deep sleep to come upon the rest of the castle: The king and queen slumbered in the throne room; the maids in the kitchen slept by the stove, where the fire flickered out; the horses in the stable, the dogs in the yard, even the flies on the wall—all went to sleep. Not a leaf stirred. Then the fairies caused great trees and brambles to spring up all around the castle.

A hundred years passed and one day a handsome prince rode by. Through all the overgrown bushes and trees he could just barely see the castle. Just then, as if by magic, the bushes and brambles parted. Curious, the prince walked toward the castle. He entered it and came to the room where the sleeping princess lay. She was so beautiful that he knelt and kissed her. At once she awoke and smiled lovingly at the handsome prince. At that moment the spell was broken and everyone in the castle awoke. The prince asked the princess for her hand in marriage and she accepted. After they were wed, Sleeping Beauty and the handsome prince rode off on a beautiful white horse to the prince's kingdom, where they lived long and happy lives together.

The Three Little Pigs

There once were three little pigs who lived in a house with their mother. One day their mother said, "It is time for you to go out into the world and take care of yourselves." Before they left, the mother pig told them to work hard and be good little pigs and most of all to look out for the big bad wolf.

The pigs went on their way. Each decided to build a house for himself. The first little pig decided to build his house of straw. "Straw is easy to work with and I shall have plenty of time to play," he said.

The second little pig decided to use twigs for his house. "There are plenty of twigs around here. I shall be able to build my house quickly and have plenty of time to play," he said.

The third little pig said, "I want my home to be nice and strong so I shall use bricks for my house." Brick houses are hard to build, and it took the third little pig a long time to finish his house. While his brothers laughed and played, he worked and worked. Finally his house was finished too.

One day the big bad wolf came. He chased the first little pig until the pig ran into his house of straw. "Little pig, little pig, let me come in," said the wolf. "Not by the hair of my chinny chin chin," cried the pig in a trembling voice. "Then I'll huff and I'll puff and I'll blow your house in!" shouted the wolf. And he did.

The first little pig ran to the house made of twigs that belonged to his brother. The wolf followed and said, "Little pigs, little pigs, let me come in." The two frightened pigs called back, "Not by the hair of our chinny chin chins." So the wolf huffed and he puffed and he blew the twig house in.

Now both little pigs ran for their lives and reached the third pig's house just in time. Their brother let them in and bolted the thick door of his sturdy brick house. Just then they heard the wolf's voice at the door. "Little pigs, little pigs, let me come in," he growled, "or I'll huff and I'll puff and I'll blow your house in!"

"Not by the hair of our chinny chin chins!" cried the pigs. So the wolf huffed and he puffed. But the house stood firm. He huffed and he puffed some more and still he could not blow the brick house in.

Then the wolf decided to get into the house by going down the chimney. But the pigs were ready. They had a huge pot of boiling water in the fireplace. When the wolf slid down the chimney, he fell right into the pot! That was the end of the wolf and the end of the three little pigs' troubles.

From that day on, they worked hard and were good little pigs, just as their mother had told them to be, and they lived happily ever after.

Rapunzel

Once a husband and wife lived happily near a great forest. One day the wife became ill. All she desired was an herb called rapunzel, which grew in the garden next door. She begged her husband to get some for her.

No one dared enter the garden because it belonged to a powerful witch. But the husband loved his wife and did not want to see her suffer, so he crept inside the garden walls. To his horror, the witch caught him. "Have mercy," the man begged. "Take whatever you please," said the witch, "but in return, I want your first-born child." And so the frightened man agreed. A year later, when a baby girl was born to the couple, the witch took her away.

The witch named the baby Rapunzel. She grew into a lovely girl. The witch kept her deep in the forest, in a high tower with no staircase or door. Rapunzel was content and often sang to herself as she sat at the window. The witch visited her every day. Standing on the ground, she called, "Rapunzel! Rapunzel! Let down your hair!" Rapunzel's hair was so long that it fell to the ground from the high window and the witch could climb up it into the tower.

One day a prince was riding through the forest when he heard the witch call "Rapunzel! Rapunzel! Let down your hair!" and saw her climb up into the tower. After the witch left, the prince called, "Rapunzel! Rapunzel! Let down your hair!" The long hair came tumbling down and the prince climbed up it to find the most beautiful girl he had ever seen. After that, the prince visited often.

The witch would never have known of the visits if Rapunzel had not said one day, as the witch climbed up, "I wish you could climb as fast as the prince."

"So the prince visits you!" cried the witch. In a fury she cut off Rapunzel's hair. Then she took Rapunzel to a faraway forest and left her there alone. The witch returned to the tower. The next day, when the prince called "Rapunzel! Rapunzel! Let down your hair!" the witch lowered Rapunzel's hair. The prince climbed up and found the angry witch instead of Rapunzel. "You will never see Rapunzel again!" she screamed. In grief the prince leaped from the window and landed in sharp thorns that blinded him.

For many years the prince wandered through the forest searching for his beloved Rapunzel. One day he heard singing. It was Rapunzel! When Rapunzel saw him, she fell into his arms and wept. Her tears fell on the prince's eyes and healed them. Then the prince took Rapunzel back to his kingdom and they lived happily ever after.

Once upon a time there lived three goats who were known as the three billy goats Gruff. They liked to go across the valley to a beautiful meadow filled with sweet grass. In order to get there the billy goats had to cross a bridge. Under the bridge lived an ugly, bad-tempered troll who would eat anyone he caught on the bridge. Usually the three billy goats Gruff quietly crossed the bridge when the troll slept.

One day the troll was awake and heard a light trip-trap, trip-trap on the wooden planks over his head. "Who is crossing my bridge?" shouted the troll.

A tiny voice answered, "It is I, the littlest billy goat Gruff."

"Well, I'm coming up to eat you!" growled the troll.

"Oh, no," begged the littlest billy goat, "I am so small. Wait for my brother who will be coming along soon. He is much bigger than I am."

"Very well," huffed the troll, and he sat down to wait for the next billy goat. Soon he heard another trip-trap. "Who goes there?" shouted the troll.

"Only I, the middle-size billy goat Gruff," was the reply.

"Good!" roared the troll. "I'm going to gobble you up!"

"Why don't you wait for my big brother?" said the middle-size billy goat Gruff. "He'll make a fine dinner."

The troll grumbled, but he allowed the second billy goat Gruff to cross the bridge. Then he waited. After a while the troll heard a very loud trip-trap, trip-trap above him. "Who is that stomping across my bridge?" bellowed the troll.

"It is I, Big Billy Goat Gruff!" came the shouted reply.

"Fine!" yelled the troll. "I've been waiting to eat you!"

"Well, come along then," answered the big billy goat loudly.

And when the troll jumped up onto the bridge, the big billy goat lowered his horns and butted the troll right back off again into the river, where he drowned.

And from that day on, the three billy goats Gruff crossed the bridge whenever they pleased and they all grew very fat indeed.

Once upon a time, in a faraway kingdom, there was a beautiful young girl who lived with her stepmother and two stepsisters. The mean, ugly stepsisters were jealous of the girl's beauty, so they made her dress in rags and dust and clean their house. They made the girl sleep near the fireplace, so she was often covered with cinders. That is why the stepsisters called her Cinderella.

One day the prince of the kingdom decided to give a ball so he could meet all the ladies of the land and choose a bride from among them. When the stepsisters received their invitation, they became very excited and talked of little else.

Finally the great day arrived. The stepsisters wore glittering new gowns and had put on all their best jewels. Cinderella was ordered to do their hair because she was very good at such things. So kind was Cinderella that she tried her best to make the stepsisters look beautiful. When it came time for them to leave, Cinderella said, "I wish I were going too."

Laughing scornfully, the stepsisters said, "You can't go in your torn, dirty dress." Then they swept haughtily out the door.

Cinderella ran into the garden and wept. "Oh, how I wish I could go to the ball," she sobbed.

"And so you shall," said a gentle voice.

Cinderella whirled around to see her fairy godmother with a wand in her hand. "You are a good and gentle girl and I shall see that you get to the ball," her fairy godmother said. "Now bring me the biggest pumpkin you can find in the garden." When Cinderella returned, the fairy godmother touched the pumpkin with her wand and it turned into a beautiful golden coach. Next she told Cinderella to fetch the mousetrap in the kitchen. The six mice within became six magnificent white horses. Then the fairy godmother told Cinderella to catch six lizards behind the garden wall. The lizards were transformed into splendid footmen.

Last, she waved her wand over Cinderella's head. In a flash Cinderella's dirty rags became a beautiful silk gown trimmed with sparkling jewels. On her feet were dainty glass slippers.

"Have a wonderful time at the ball," said the fairy godmother, "but remember that when the clock strikes twelve, the magic ends and everything will be as before. You must leave the ball before midnight."

When Cinderella arrived at the palace everyone looked at her in wonder, especially the prince, so dazzling was she. For the rest of the evening he danced only with her. Cinderella was so happy that she forgot all about the time. Then the clock struck the first chime of midnight. "I must go!" cried Cinderella as she ran out of the ballroom. As she fled down the palace steps she lost one of her glass slippers.

The next day the prince, having found the slipper, went from house to house to find the girl to whom it belonged. But it fitted no one. Cinderella's house was the last one he tried. The stepsisters tried in vain to fit their large feet inside the tiny slipper. But it was no use. Then Cinderella stepped forward and said, "May I try?"

The stepsisters laughed and said, "Don't be silly. You weren't even at the palace."

But the prince insisted that everyone in the kingdom try on the slipper. He tried it on Cinderella. It slid easily onto her tiny foot. Then, to everyone's astonishment, she reached into her apron pocket and pulled out the matching slipper. The prince was overjoyed and took Cinderella immediately to the palace, where they were married. Cinderella was so good-hearted that she even forgave her stepsisters for their meanness. Then she brought them to the palace where they all lived happily ever after.